T 6734

292                                    $9.00

Richardson, I.M.

THE RETURN OF ODYSSEUS

13310   PTA 97

6734   DEMCO

The Return of Odysseus

Tales from the Odyssey

Written by I. M. Richardson
Illustrated by Hal Frenck

Troll Associates

Library of Congress Cataloging in Publication Data

Richardson, I. M.
    The return of Odysseus.

    (Tales from the Odyssey / adapted by I. M. Richardson;
bk. 6)
    Summary: Odysseus returns at last to Ithaca where he
rids his house of the evil suitors, is reunited with
Penelope, and visits his aging, grieving father.
    [1. Mythology, Greek] I. Frenck, Hal, ill.
II. Homer. Odyssey. III. Title. IV. Series:
Richardson, I. M. Tales from the Odyssey; bk. 6.
PZ8.1.R396Tal 1984 bk. 6   292'.13s [292'.13]   83-14234
ISBN 0-8167-0015-X (lib. bdg.)
ISBN 0-8167-0016-8 (pbk.)

Odysseus was King of Ithaca and hero of the Trojan War. Nearly ten years earlier, he had left Troy with a fleet of ships, but he had not yet reached home. Poseidon, the angry god of the sea, had delayed him time after time. Finally, Odysseus had been washed ashore on an island.

The king and queen of the island listened to the tales of
Odysseus. Their guest told how he had blinded the Cyclops,
who was the son of Poseidon. He also told of terrible
storms, of man-eating giants, and of monsters too terrible to
imagine. Then the king and queen showered their visitor
with gifts of all kinds. They promised to send him home on
their fastest ship.

When the gifts were loaded on board, the crew rowed the ship out to sea. As the wind filled the sails, Odysseus fell into a sound sleep on the deck. All day and all through the night, they sailed on. When morning dawned, they were approaching the island of Ithaca.

They entered a sheltered harbor and gently beached the ship. Odysseus did not awaken. The sailors carried him to the beach and placed him beneath an olive tree. When they had piled his gifts on the shore, they went back to the ship. Then they left the harbor and headed home.

Poseidon was not pleased. He was already angry with Odysseus for blinding the Cyclops. Now his anger grew worse. "Those sailors must be punished for helping that wicked man," he growled. So just as they entered their home port, he turned their entire ship to solid stone.

When Odysseus awoke on the shores of Ithaca, he was not alone. Athena, the goddess of wisdom, was with him. She helped him hide his gifts inside a cave. Then she said, "Your house has been overrun by unruly suitors—men who wish to marry Penelope, your faithful wife. They are devouring your food and wrecking your home."

Odysseus replied, "I will soon have my revenge upon
them." Then Athena disguised him as a beggar, and said,
"Go to the hut of the old man who tends your pigs and
hogs. Even after all these years, that swineherder is loyal
to you. I will go and get your son, Telemachos. He is in
Sparta, seeking news of your fate."

Athena went to Sparta and told Telemachos to return home at once. "But be careful," she said. "Some of the wicked suitors plan to ambush you in the narrow strait that leads to Ithaca. So instead of using that route, you must go around the island and land on the other side. Then go directly to the old swineherder's hut."

When Telemachos arrived at the swineherder's hut, the old man greeted him warmly. Ever since Odysseus had left for the Trojan War, the swineherder had been like a father to Telemachos. Of course, the young man did not know that his father was the stranger in beggar's rags who sat in the swineherder's hut.

Odysseus waited until he was alone with Telemachos. Then he removed his disguise. "I know you do not recognize me," he said, "because you were only a baby when I left home. But I am Odysseus—your father." At this, Telemachos cried out, "Father! You have come home at last!" Then they threw their arms around each other.

Odysseus told his son of the many exciting adventures of the past ten years. Then he told him what he planned to do. "You must tell no one that I have returned," said Odysseus. "Dressed as a beggar, I will mingle among the suitors. When the moment is right, I will reveal my true identity. Then we shall have our revenge."

Telemachos returned to the palace. He told his mother he
had learned that Odysseus was being held captive on an
island in the sea. At this bad news, Penelope's face grew
pale. But a prophet spoke out, saying, "You must heed my
words. Odysseus is here in Ithaca, planning the destruction
of the wicked suitors." Now Penelope did not know what
to believe.

As the suitors entered the great hall in the palace, Penelope left by another door. Soon Odysseus arrived, dressed in rags. He began begging food from the suitors. One of them picked up a footstool and threw it at him. Odysseus ducked and said, "You think you will court Penelope and win her hand. But I think you will be *buried* before you are *married*."

A little later, the town beggar came into the hall. Of course, he did not know that the other man in rags was Odysseus. "Get out of here at once," he boasted, "or I'll throw you out myself!" But Odysseus replied, "There is plenty for both of us." Then the town beggar flew into a rage. Before long, the suitors had formed a ring around the two ragged men.

Odysseus tucked up his rags, so he would not trip on them. Now the town beggar could see the bulging muscles, and he was filled with fear. But the suitors pushed him into the ring anyway. With one mighty blow, Odysseus knocked him senseless. Then he dragged him outside and propped him up against the wall, like a scarecrow.

At this point, Penelope entered the dining hall. Athena had made her so beautiful that the suitors were dazzled by her loveliness. "Each of you wishes to marry me," she said. "Yet, instead of acting like gentlemen, you are behaving like pigs! If you hope to win my favor, you should be showering me with gifts, not devouring all my food."

"We will bring you gifts," the suitors replied. "We will give you the most valuable treasures we have. But we will not give up until you marry one of us!" Then they brought magnificent gifts of gold and jewels and heaped them in front of her. Penelope turned and left the hall. Her maids followed her, carrying away the treasures.

That night, after the suitors had left the great hall, Penelope returned. She thought the stranger in rags might have heard some news of Odysseus. "Have you seen my husband in your travels?" she asked. And he replied, "I have not seen Odysseus for many years, but I believe he will be home soon." Penelope sighed, and said, "How I wish that could be true."

Then a faithful old nurse began to bathe the visitor's feet, to make him comfortable. As she washed him, she recognized a certain scar that Odysseus had received when he was a boy. She knew at once who he was, but Odysseus swore her to silence. Penelope had seen nothing.

"My heart tells me to wait for the return of Odysseus," Penelope said. "On the other hand, the suitors will give me no peace until I marry one of them. I am so confused! I once dreamed that my husband would return and kill all the suitors. But I fear that dream will never come true. So tomorrow, I will announce an archery contest, and the winner shall become my husband."

The next day, she went to the storage room where her husband's treasures were kept. There she found his bow and arrows, which would be used in the archery contest. As she took the bow from its case, she began to weep, for it reminded her of her lost husband. Then she dried her tears, and took the bow and arrows to the great hall.

When she stood before the suitors, she called out, "Listen to me! Is there anyone among you who can string this bow? And can he shoot a single arrow through a row of twelve axheads? If so, then I will marry him." Telemachos lined up the axheads so their holes were all in a row. But none of the suitors could even bend the bow far enough to fasten the string!

When Penelope had left the hall, Odysseus stepped forward. "Let a poor old beggar try," he said. He picked up the huge bow. With no effort at all, he bent the mighty weapon and hooked the string over the end. Then he picked up an arrow and took aim. It went whistling through all twelve axheads, straight and true.

Then Odysseus threw off his beggar's disguise. He let another arrow fly, and it cut down the leader of the suitors. "Who are you?" cried the others, who still did not recognize Odysseus. He picked up a third arrow and said, "My odyssey is over, and I have returned home just in time. Now you shall all pay for your wickedness!"

Then they knew who he was, and they turned pale with fear. They tried to blame their fallen companion, but it was no use. A great battle followed. There were more than a hundred suitors, but Odysseus had Athena and Zeus on his side. Before long, all the suitors had paid with their lives.

Now the old nurse told her mistress that Odysseus had returned. "I have seen the scar he received when he was a boy," she said. But Penelope still would not believe he was really her husband. She decided to put him to a secret test. "Come with me," she said. "Help me move our bed a bit closer to the window, where there is more breeze."

When he heard this, Odysseus cried out, "Woman! Have you gone mad? You know that our bed can never be moved. One of its posts is carved from a living olive tree, so it is rooted in its place." Odysseus was the only man who knew this secret. Now Penelope was sure that her husband had returned. She ran into his arms, and they embraced.

But the story of Odysseus does not end there. He had yet to be reunited with his aging father. The old man lived on a farm in the country, where he was slowly dying of grief for his missing son. When Odysseus arrived at the farm, the old man was dressed in ragged clothes, and was wearing a goatskin hat.

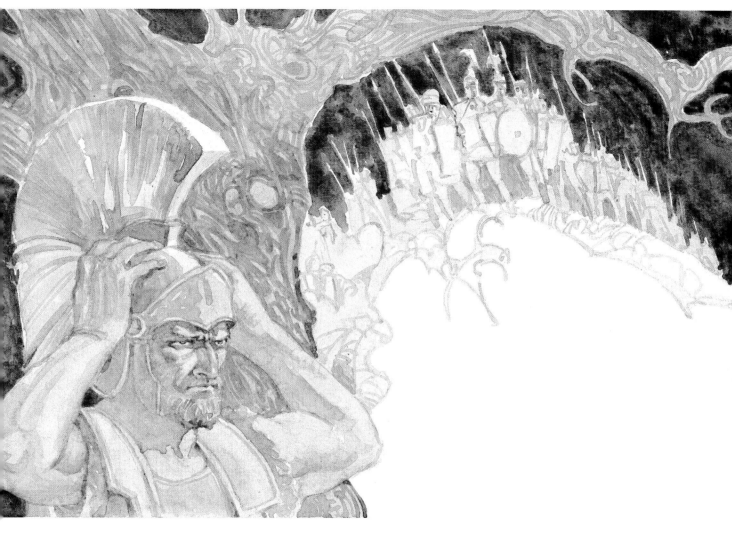

Odysseus embraced him for the first time in many long years, and said, "Father, I am home. I have killed the evil suitors." But the families of some of the dead suitors had vowed to seek revenge. Across the fields they came, armed and angry. Again Odysseus prepared for battle.

But Athena came down from Mount Olympus and quieted the crowds. "Lay down your arms," she said, "and bury your anger along with your dead." From then on, peace reigned throughout the land. Odysseus, the King of Ithaca, had returned home at last.